Stories for Christmas

Selected and edited by
SALLY GRINDLEY

Illustrated by
HELEN COOPER

SMITHMARK

For Vanessa

First published in 1990 by Kingfisher Books
First published in the United States in 1991
by SMITHMARK Publishers Inc.,
112 Madison Avenue, New York, NY 10016.

SMITHMARK books are available for bulk purchase
for sales promotion and premium use. For details
write or telephone the Manager of Special Sales,
SMITHMARK Publishers Inc., 112 Madison Avenue,
New York, NY 10016. (212) 532-6600.

Printed in Hong Kong

For permission to reproduce copyright material, acknowledgement and thanks are
due to Heinemann Children's Books and Lothrop, Lee and Shephard (a division
of William Morrow & Co.) for "Wake Up, Bear ... It's Christmas!" by Stephen
Gammell. The other stories appear for the first time in this collection.
Permissions granted by the authors.

CONTENTS

WAKE UP, BEAR...
IT'S CHRISTMAS!

Stephen Gammell

As the last few leaves of autumn fell, Bear was padding down his walking trail. He was going home for his winter's sleep. But he wasn't going to be sleeping all winter.

"That's right," he said, as he reached his door. "I've missed it now for seven years, and seems I've heard it said that it's a happy, joyful time, but I'm always in bed. Well, this year things are different. I've decided what to do. I'm getting up for Christmas, instead of sleeping through!"

After setting his clock and fixing his bed, Bear blew out the candle. Feeling happy but tired, he snuggled down under his blanket.

"Well," he yawned, "when I wake up I wonder what I'll see. Anyway, I hope it's fun when Christmas comes to . . ."

He fell asleep.

The weeks went by. The forest was still and silent. The only sound was the wind as it blew softly during the day, and harder at night.

The snow started to fall late one afternoon. It fell gently at first, then became heavier. Soon, snow covered nearly everything in the forest. It almost came up to Bear's window.

Bear slept.

The clock woke him late one wintry afternoon. Sitting up slowly, Bear rubbed his eyes. Then he remembered it was Christmas Eve! His nose was cold as he smelled the fresh snow.

Putting on his scarf and mittens, he went out into the woods, where he found a nice little pine tree. Back home in the candlelight, he decorated his tree. He got an old

stocking from his cupboard, and hung it up by his window. Then humming a little tune, Bear fixed his blanket and sat back with his guitar to enjoy the evening.

"There. Everything looks cosy now, and festive, I believe. I'm so glad I'm wide awake tonight, on Christmas Eve."

He had not been sitting long when he heard a tapping sound at his door. Just a branch in the winter wind, he thought. But then he heard it again. It was a knock. Before Bear could move, the door opened.

"Hello, Bear. I saw your light. I'll warm myself, if that's all right?"

Delighted by this unexpected visitor, Bear got up and invited him in.

"Well, hello stranger, come on in. Don't stand out there

and freeze. It's warm inside and you can rest — here, take my blanket, please. I'm only playing my guitar and looking at my tree. But if you've nowhere else to go, do spend some time with me."

So they sat, Bear and his visitor, talking about the snow and the wind, singing a few tunes, and enjoying Christmas Eve. Finally, the little fellow, who was now quite warm, stood and said he really must be going.

"I thank you, Bear, for all you've done. This really has been lots of fun."

Bear stood in the doorway and watched him go off through the forest, thinking what a nice time it had been. All of a sudden his friend shouted back at him.

"Come for a ride, Bear, come with me. I'd really like your company."

A ride! On Christmas Eve! Bear grabbed his scarf and mittens and ran through the deep snow to where a big sleigh sat waiting. The little driver turned as Bear reached the sleigh.

"Just climb up here and hang on tight. You'll be back home before it's light."

Wrapping the big quilt around him, Bear sat down in the seat. Before he could say "LET'S BE OFF," they were off!

Off and up! Up through the air and away into the snowy night . . .

"Oh, what a Christmas!" hollered Bear. "I've never had such fun. I'd like to think that it could be like this for everyone. But most of all, just meeting you has really brought me cheer. Why don't we plan, my little friend, to do this every year?"

So off they flew, far in the night and through the swirling snow, with Bear's companion laughing loud a jolly HO HO HO!

AND THERE WERE SHEPHERDS

Mary Rayner

And there were shepherds that night out on the hills looking after their sheep. The angel of the Lord appeared to them and told them that Jesus was born, and where they would find him. And there was light all about, and suddenly many, many angels, and more and more, all praising God and singing, "Glory be to God on high, Gloria, Gloria."

The sheep were huddled together in fright on the bare hillside. The great white light was fading now, and the voices gone. Below them the little group of shepherds was stamping out the embers of the fire.

The ewes watched. They couldn't believe what they saw. The shepherds were leaving, going off down the hill. They picked up the lamb with the hurt foot and carried him with them. The dog followed.

"Well!" said the first sheep.

9

"Going off without even seeing that we're all right. I don't think much of that!" said the second.

"Shepherds nowadays. Don't know their job. Off on some jaunt without so much as a word or a by your leave! No thought for others . . ." said the third.

"What about us? What if a wolf comes?" said the fourth, and they all looked over their shoulders into the dark, and huddled closer.

"Not up to it, that's what I say. Shouldn't ever have been hired," said the fifth. "It's all very well, all this *Gloria* nonsense, but who's going to look after us, that's what I'd like to know?"

"*And* they've taken my lamb," said the sixth. "And him with a bad foot."

"They could have left the dog at least," said the seventh. "But no, they've taken him as well."

"Typical," said the eighth. "People! You can't trust them an inch. One word from on high, and they're off on some fool's errand, responsibilities forgotten, all of us left to the wolves . . ."

She knelt on her front knees, and lurched down on to the ground. The others did the same, settling down around her, still grumbling. They waited in a tight little knot, every now and then eyeing the scatter of rocks where a wolf might be lurking.

The night was very dark, the stars brilliant. For the sheep it was a long wait until the first pale light showed above the hills in the east, and they could be easy. The day had dawned, and nothing had happened to them after all.

The sun rose higher, but no one came. The sheep wandered across the hillside, their bells tinkling, searching for grass among the dry rocks.

At last, about noon, they heard the barking of the dog, and behind him they saw the shepherds. The lamb could just be made out, following them.

The sheep trotted down the hill. The lamb bounded toward them, bleating in excitement.

"You'll never believe what I saw. All the way to Bethlehem we went, and into a stable, and there was a baby, and its mother, and her husband, and some cattle, and a donkey, and we all prayed —"

"Now just a minute, young fellow," said the ewe who was his mother. "Slow up."

"What d'you mean, prayed?" asked the first ewe. "Who to?"

"To God, of course," said the lamb simply. "It was a sign. The angels said so. The baby. A Savior, Christ the Lord."

"Well I never," said the second ewe.

"Maybe that's why no wolves came last night," said the third ewe.

"I take it all back," said the fifth ewe.

"They were right to go after all," said the eighth, and they all nodded their heads, bleating. The bells clonked and tinkled across the hillside.

"And my foot's better," said the lamb, holding it up.

IMELDA
AND THE
DRAGON

Martin Waddell

Once there was a lonely Dragon.

It was lonely because it didn't meet many people, and
when it did it toasted them, and then it ate them, which is
how Dragons stop people from stealing their Dragon gold.

One Christmas Day, the Dragon was out for a walk when
it saw a village, so it thought it would toast the people and
eat them. Puff-puff-puff! it went, warming up. The people
saw the puffs, and they all ran away.

All except Imelda. Imelda thought that she *might* like the

Dragon. She didn't know for sure, because the Dragon only came around every ten years or so, and Imelda was only seven. She stayed where she was.

PUFF-PUFF-PUFF! Out of the snowy woods came the Dragon. It was big and green and scary, with a long tail and little fat wings. It came waddling up to Imelda, in a big cloud of smoke.

"Merry Christmas, Dragon!" said Imelda.

The Dragon heard someone squeak, from down there between its webby feet, but it wasn't able to see Imelda because of the smoke.

"Er . . . Merry Christmas," it said. Then it thought a bit. "What is Christmas?" it asked.

"It's when people are kind to each other, and give each

other presents," said Imelda. "It's *now*. This is Christmas Day."

"Nobody is ever kind to me," said the Dragon. "Nobody ever gives me presents. People don't like Dragons."

Just then, Imelda's Mom came running up to rescue Imelda from the Dragon. She was all dressed up in a suit of armor she had borrowed and she was waving a broad-sword.

"Oh, good-eee! A fight!" said the Dragon, and it got ready to toast her.

"Stop!" cried Imelda. "I'm Imelda and that's my Mom. I need my Mom and I don't want her toasted."

"Toasting people is what Dragons do!" said the Dragon.

"Maybe that is *why* people don't like Dragons," said Imelda, who wasn't so sure about liking Dragons any more herself.

"Do you think people would like me if I was kind?" asked the Dragon.

"Yes," said Imelda. "Try it."

"How do I begin?" asked the Dragon.

"Wish my Mom a Merry Christmas," suggested Imelda.

"Er...Merry Christmas, Imelda's Mom," said the Dragon.

"And a Merry Christmas to you, Dragon," said Imelda's Mom, lowering her broadsword instead of whacking the Dragon with it, which wouldn't have done much good anyway, because the Dragon was too tough.

"Now give my Mom a present," whispered Imelda.

And the Dragon gave Imelda's Mom some of its gold.

"The Dragon is giving away gold!" all the villagers cried, and they came out of hiding and rushed into the village.

"Merry Christmas, Dragon!" they all cheered.

"Can I toast them?" said the Dragon.

"No," said Imelda. "Not at Christmas."

"Oh, all right!" said the Dragon, and it wished all the villagers a Merry Christmas and gave them gold too.

"What a kind Dragon!" the villagers cried, and they started talking to the Dragon. They said how nice it was to meet a kind Dragon for a change, and they even gave it Christmas presents that they thought a Dragon might enjoy — like firelighters and matches and kindling in case its fire went out, and blocks of ice for times when it got overheated. The village children climbed up on the Dragon and had Dragon rides, and they tickled it and made it laugh.

It was the best Christmas party the Dragon had ever been to. It was the first one, as well.

"I wish it could be Christmas every day!" the Dragon said, when the party was over and everybody was cleaning up.

"Why?" said Imelda.

"So people would like me and be friends," said the Dragon.

Imelda thought for a bit.

"You could *pretend* it was Christmas Day every day," she told the Dragon. "Then you could be Christmas-kind to everyone instead of toasting them, and they would be Christmas-kind to you."

So that's what the Dragon did. It wasn't a nasty Dragon any more, and it never toasted anybody or ate them ever again. All thanks to Imelda . . . and Christmas.

NOT *QUITE* CHRISTMAS

Dyan Sheldon

The streets were decked with tinsel and colored lights. The shops were decorated with angels and reindeer and laughing elves. Santa Claus was everywhere.

Belinda wanted to celebrate Christmas too.

"Don't be silly," said Belinda's mother. "We don't celebrate Christmas. It's not our holiday."

But Belinda wanted to give presents. She wanted to make cookies shaped like stars. She wanted to sing carols. She wanted a Christmas tree. A Christmas tree covered with bright balls and winking lights. A tree with an angel right at its top. "But everybody celebrates Christmas," said Belinda.

"No they don't," said her mother. "Everyone has different holidays."

Belinda frowned. "Well, it *seems* like everyone celebrates Christmas."

"What about Uncle Frank?" asked Belinda's mother. "He doesn't celebrate Christmas. And my friend Sandra and her family? And your friend Emily across the street? And that nice doctor who took care of you when you were ill last summer? None of them celebrate Christmas either."

"Well everybody else does," said Belinda.

"Don't pay any attention," said Belinda's mother.

"It's hard not to," said Belinda.

Belinda's mother looked thoughtful.

"We could just have a tree," said Belinda. "It wouldn't have to be a big tree."

"There are plenty of trees outside," said Belinda's mother. "Where they belong."

Belinda went to school. The class was making paper chains. "Have you got your tree yet?" asked Amy.

Belinda wondered what she was going to do with her chain. "No," said Belinda, "not yet."

"I'm going to make my mother a special box to keep her pens in for Christmas," said David.

"I'm making my mother a vase," said Amy. "What are you making for your mother, Belinda?"

"I haven't decided," said Belinda.

"I'm asking Santa Claus to bring me a skateboard," said Amy. "What are you asking him to bring you?"

"I want a new bike," said David.

"What about you, Belinda?" asked Amy.

Belinda said, "I think my chain's too long."

Belinda and her mother and father were watching television. Three polar bears in Santa Claus hats were singing about Christmas.

"You're very quiet tonight, Belinda," said Belinda's father.

"Um," said Belinda.

"What's wrong?" asked her father.

"Nothing," said Belinda.

"What's that red and green thing in the wastebasket?" asked Belinda's mother.

"Nothing," said Belinda.

Belinda's mother lifted out Belinda's paper chain. "It doesn't look like nothing," she said.

"It's just something dumb we made at school."

Belinda's father said, "Oh."

Belinda's mother leaned over and whispered to him. "She's upset because we don't celebrate Christmas."

Belinda's father said, "Ah."

It was Christmas Eve. There was no one to play with. No one to watch a video with. Everybody was getting ready for Christmas. Except for Belinda. She sat looking out of the window at the falling snow.

"Are you going to sit there looking out of the window all day?" asked her mother. "Maybe," said Belinda.

"Why don't you go out and play?" asked her mother.

"I don't feel like it," said Belinda.

"I know. Why don't you take out your sled?"

"I don't feel like it," said Belinda.

"Why don't you watch a video then?"

"I don't feel like it," said Belinda.

"I know," said Belinda's mother. "Why don't you help me make some cookies?"

"Cookies?" said Belinda.

"Yes," said Belinda's mother. "I have some red and green sugar we could sprinkle on top."

"You mean like Christmas cookies?" asked Belinda.

Belinda's mother smiled. "Not quite," she said.

Belinda's father came through the front door. "Something smells good," he called.

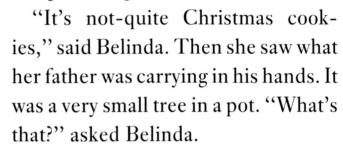

"It's not-quite Christmas cookies," said Belinda. Then she saw what her father was carrying in his hands. It was a very small tree in a pot. "What's that?" asked Belinda.

"It's a bay tree," said Belinda's father. "It was on sale in the supermarket." He put it on the table in front of the window. "I thought it would look pretty with your paper chain on it."

"Oh, and you know what?" said Belinda's mother. "I think I have some bows that would look nice on it as well."

"And how about hanging a cookie or two on it?" asked Belinda's father. "That would brighten it up."

Belinda looked at her mother. Then Belinda looked at her father. "You mean decorate it like a Christmas tree?" she asked.

"Well, not quite," said Belinda's father.

It was Christmas Day. Belinda's father was sitting in the living room, looking at the not-quite Christmas tree.

"You know," he said, "it looks very pretty. Especially with your chain. It's a shame there isn't anyone else to see it."

"You know," said Belinda's mother, "that's almost exactly what I was thinking. We have all those delicious cookies Belinda and I made and no one to help us eat them."

"I've an idea," said Belinda's father. "Why don't we invite some friends over to share them with us?"

"Because everybody's busy celebrating Christmas today," said Belinda glumly.

"Not everybody," said Belinda's mother. "There's Uncle Frank, and Sandra and her family, and Emily and her family, and that nice doctor who took care of you when you were ill last summer ..."

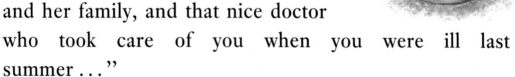

Belinda was having a wonderful time. The living room was full of people. They were all eating cookies and drinking punch and playing games. The doctor who had taken care of Belinda when she was ill last summer was telling jokes. Everyone was laughing.

"And look what I found in the attic," said Belinda's mother hurrying into the room. "Colored lights from Belinda's birthday!"

"Perfect!" said Belinda's father. "We can put them on the tree."

Everyone stood in a circle to watch.

"Isn't that beautiful!" everyone cried when the lights went on.

"Oh, isn't this a lovely party," said Emily.

"It's the best party I've ever been to," said Sandra.

"Me too," said the doctor.

"Why, it's almost like a Christmas party," smiled Uncle Frank.

"Oh no, Uncle Frank," said Belinda. "Not quite."

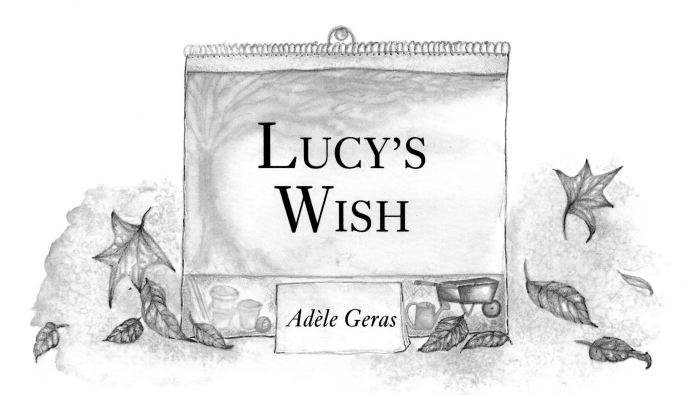

LUCY'S WISH

Adèle Geras

Every day Lucy watched the leaves falling from the trees in the garden and every day she asked her mother or sister or father what date it was, hoping that the answer would be Christmas Day.

One day, she asked her question in the supermarket as her mother was pushing her around in the shopping cart.

"It's only October the 23rd," said Lucy's mother, "but we're making the Christmas cake today."

Lucy smiled. She loved getting ready for Christmas.

At home, Lucy helped her mother prepare everything she needed to make the cake. Apart from the flour and eggs and sugar and margarine, there were all the packages they had bought in the supermarket: raisins, currants, sultanas, cherries, mixed peel, and slivered almonds. Lucy put some of them into the bowl, and at the end she had to stir the squelchy beige mixture that was full of unexpected bits and lumps. As she stirred, she had to make a wish.

"What did you wish for?" Mom asked Lucy.

"That's a secret," said Lucy. "The wish doesn't work if you tell anyone what it is."

After the cake was made, days and days went by and nothing at all was said about Christmas. Outside in the garden, the trees were bare of leaves.

"What's the date?" asked Lucy.

"November the 30th," said her sister, Frances, who was eight. "I think we ought to start making the Christmas decorations."

"Yes, let's," said Lucy.

So Lucy and Frances sat in the kitchen with a big jar of paste and lots of colored paper, and made snakes of paper chains to go around the walls. All afternoon they sat at the big table by the window. The houses across the road grew darker and darker, until they looked like black paper cutouts against the sky that turned pink as the sun went down, then mauve, then blue.

"Look," said Frances. "There's the first star. Make a wish, quickly."

Lucy closed her eyes and wished.

"What did you wish?" asked Frances.

"It's a secret," said Lucy. "The wish doesn't work if you tell anyone what it is."

After the decorations had been made, counting the days

to Christmas was easier. Lucy and Frances each had an Advent calendar, and every day they each opened a small door and looked at the picture inside. On December the 19th, Lucy's Dad said:

"I've got the Christmas tree in the garage. Time to go and get all that stuff from the attic to put on it."

So Lucy and Frances and their Dad went up into the attic to find the boxes full of what Lucy called the Tree Jewels. They brought the boxes downstairs and hung thin balls of shiny silver and purple and midnight blue from the

branches. They looped golden tinsel around the tree, tied red ribbons into bows with long, trailing ends, and balanced small, silver-paper-covered stars and moon shapes among the dark pine needles.

"Lucy," said Dad, "I'll hold you up while you put the angel on top here. Don't forget to make a wish, now."

Lucy closed her eyes and wished. "What did you wish for?" asked Dad.

"It's a secret," said Lucy. "The wish doesn't work if you tell anyone what it is."

On Christmas Eve, Lucy couldn't sleep.

"Why can't you sleep?" asked Frances.

"I'm sad," said Lucy.

"How can you be sad on Christmas Eve?"

"I'm sad because my wish didn't come true. Even though I wished for it three times."

"What did you wish for?" asked Frances.

"It was silly. I don't want to say." Lucy turned her face into the pillow.

"Well, go to sleep now," said Frances. "It's Christmas Day tomorrow. You'll be happy then."

Lucy thought about her wish. Perhaps it really had been

silly to hope that the garden, which was full of fallen leaves and bare trees and dark earth, could be made pretty again. Lucy knew that leaves and flowers came in the spring, but it seemed unfair to her that when everything *inside* was so bright and beautiful the garden should be so gray and empty.

"Maybe," she thought, "I'll try again. Just once more." Lucy closed her eyes and wished. Then she fell asleep.

In the morning, Frances woke up first.

"Lucy," she whispered. "Wake up. Let's see what's in our stockings." Lucy woke up and together the two girls ate the tangerines and nuts and raisins that someone had put into their Christmas stockings during the night.

"It's very sunny," said Frances. "You can tell even though the curtains are closed. It's so light."

"Let's open them," said Lucy. "You pull that one and I'll pull this one."

The curtains opened.

"Look!" whispered Lucy. "Oh, Frances, look! My wish came true in the night."

The garden glittered in the sun. Every branch and twig and blade of grass, every roof and windowsill, the dark brown earth and the green tops of the hedges: everything was thick with snow. The window of Lucy and Frances's bedroom had frost all around the edges of the glass, like a border of white flowers.

"It's lovely!" said Lucy. "I never thought it would look as pretty as that."

"Is that what you wished for?" asked Frances. "Did you wish for snow?"

"I didn't know I wished for it," said Lucy, "but I suppose I must have."

"What did you say, then?"

"I just closed my eyes and said: I wish the garden could be decorated for Christmas."

"Well," said Frances, "it *is* decorated. Let's go and tell Mom and Dad."

They ran into their Mom and Dad's room.

"Wake up!" said Lucy. "It's Christmas Day, and my wish came true!"

CHRISTMAS LIGHTS

Angela Bull

Christmas was coming. Amy sang *Away in a Manger* at school, and smelled mince pies cooking when she got home.

A neighbor, Mrs. Robinson, popped her head around the kitchen door. "I'm taking a load of kids into town tonight to see the Christmas lights," she said. "Would Amy like to come?"

"Yes, please," said Amy's Mom.

Mrs. Robinson collected quite a crowd; enough to fill two cars. They all lived near Amy: Zoë and her best friend Donna; Peter with the glasses, and Ian with the leather jacket; and Jenny who had long fair hair. Amy was much the smallest. There were grown-ups as well — and there was a dog. He was a sausage dog called Chips. Amy liked him at once.

It was a squash in the car. People talked and laughed above Amy's head. Chips sat on the floor. Amy could feel his smooth coat beside her knees.

The cars stopped in a big parking lot.

"Come back here if you get lost," said Mrs. Robinson to everyone. Then they scrambled out — all except Chips.

"He'd better stay here. He might get stepped on," said Mrs. Robinson. She shut the car door. Chips peeped sadly through the window.

Amy forgot about him, for the first Christmas lights swung high in the air above the parking lot entrance. All along the street they went, like a glittering necklace of red and silver beads, around a curve and out of sight.

"Come on. This is only the beginning," said Mrs. Robinson. The big children hurried ahead. Their voices floated back. "Wow!" "Brilliant!"

The grown-ups chatted together. Amy came last, following.

At a corner, where two necklaces met, a Santa Claus was

outlined in lights against the black sky. His cloak was red; his beard was white. One hand was pointing.

"He's showing us the way to go," said Mrs. Robinson.

Santa Claus after Santa Claus hung above the street, all pointing. There were colored lights in the stores they passed, and silver trees, and strings of shimmering tinsel. Amy couldn't help stopping to look at everything; and she stopped too by a stall selling hot chestnuts, which smelled delicious. But she was getting left behind. She ran along the crowded sidewalk, until she could see Ian's leather jacket again, and Jenny's long fair hair.

Suddenly, above them, was a Santa Claus without a beard. His white lights had gone out.

"Here we are," said Mrs. Robinson. "This is the square."

Everywhere, shining lights swooped and zig-zagged. Strands gathered like maypole ribbons, and swung away to distant corners. Among them flew angels on bright wings of light. Trumpeters blew silver trumpets, and drummer boys beat drums of scarlet and gold.

The tree stood in the middle. Amy had never seen such a tall one. It reached up and up, as if it were stretching to touch the flying angels and the little drummer boys. More lights spangled its branches; white ones, silver ones. Crowning it was a five-pointed golden star. Christmas carol music floated out of loudspeakers. Some people were singing along with it. Amy threaded her way through them toward the tree. The blaze of its lights dazzled her. She gazed, blinked — and then stared around.

Where was Mrs. Robinson? Where was Jenny's long hair, and Ian's leather jacket? She could only see the dark shapes of strangers, crowds of them, filling the square.

Amy's heart began to thump. Though she was surrounded by more people than she'd ever seen before, she felt horribly alone. Alone and abandoned. Lost.

"Go back to the car if you're lost," Mrs. Robinson had said. But where was the car? Amy looked all around, shaking with fright.

Five roads branched off the square. Which one led to the parking lot? Santa Clauses shone at every corner, and suddenly Amy remembered. The Santa Claus she wanted had no lights in his beard.

She saw him almost at once, pointing across at her. Feeling much happier, she ran up to him, and turned down his street, under the necklace of red and silver beads. She only had to go the way the Santa Clauses *weren't* pointing. Here was the chestnut seller, packing up his stall. Here were the stores with silver trees and tinsel. She was going to be all right. She came to the last Santa Claus. She reached the parking lot.

"Woof!" Before she had time to look for the car, she heard Chips barking. He was standing on his hind legs on the back seat. Mrs. Robinson had left the window open a crack, and his little nose was poking through the gap.

"Hello!" said Amy. She put her fingers to the crack, and Chips licked them. Then she smelled hot chestnuts. The chestnut seller, wheeling his barrow past, stopped.

"Now, dear, are you lost?" he asked.

"No," said Amy. "Just waiting."

"Here," he said. "My last bag." He dropped a paper bag of hot chestnuts into Amy's cold hands.

Amy opened the bag, peeled a chestnut, broke it in two, ate half herself, and gave Chips half through the open window. She heard his tail thump the car seat as it wagged.

And that was the nicest moment in the whole evening.

"Amy!" It was Mrs. Robinson. "Thank goodness you're here! I was so worried. I'd no idea there'd be such a crowd; and I didn't know where you'd gone."

"You said come back to the car if we were lost," Amy explained.

"You were quite right. Good girl! Thank you for being so sensible." Everyone else gathered around. Jenny smiled at Amy through her veil of long hair. The boys grinned.

Amy sat on the back seat of the car, with Chips on her knee, sharing out her chestnuts. Above them all the necklaces of lights swooped and glittered; but it was time to go home.

KING WOD'S SURPRISE PRESENT

Chris Powling

King Wod was very, very rich.

He had so much money he could have filled up the stocking of every kid in the land — yes, including yours if you'd been around — and still had plenty left over. So why was it he *hated* Christmas?

The reason was this. More than anything else in the world, King Wod wanted a surprise present on Christmas morning.

Is that all?

Aha...let's not forget how rich he was. Year after year it was the same. Whatever present he was given — it didn't matter how wonderful — King Wod had one already. For instance:

A horse with multi-colored hooves for riding on rainbows.

A book of answers to every question a teacher can ask.

A picnic basket that glowed in the dark when you took it on a midnight feast.

A pillow for singing you to sleep.

A special puddle for splashing indoors without wetting the carpet...

But why go on? "I've got one of those," King Wod always said.

Eventually, early one Christmas morning before the sun was even up, he lost his temper. He kicked over his royal throne, tore his royal cloak in half and sent his royal crown spinning straight through the palace window. "Can't anyone bring me a surprise present?" he roared. "Send for the royal wizard!"

"I'm already here, your majesty."

"Well don't just stand there, wizard. *Do* something. That's an order!"

ABRA - CA - ZAM!

"Eh?"

Quick as a blink, there was King Wod in a dark, snow-covered forest. "Where am I?" he asked. "The North Pole? Just wait till I get back to the palace — that wizard is in deep, deep trouble."

Right now, though, it was King Wod himself in deep, deep trouble. The snow was knee-high in some places and up to his armpits in other places and it was hard to tell one place from the other. Soon he was as stiff and chilly as an icicle. "And if I don't keep moving that's what I will be," he groaned. "A king-sized icicle. Wait, is that a house I see over there?"

With a sigh of relief he trudged toward a tiny, snow-thatched cottage on the forest's edge.

The cottage was empty.

Lived in, yes. There was a fire ready in the grate, food ready in the pantry, and comfy furniture ready in the living room. "Where's the owner, though?" asked the king. "And why are there no paper-chains and Christmas cards and a tree in the corner with colored lights?"

For there was no sign of Christmas in the cottage at all.

Except, that is, for an Advent calendar on the mantlepiece. It was open at December the 24th. "Christmas Eve," King Wod said. Somehow this made the small, snowbound cottage seem emptier than ever.

No wonder the king felt lonely. Was this to be his first ever Christmas on his own? "Better get warm for a start," he told himself. "Then keep busy. That's what I must do."

He was quite right, of course. It was fun to chop down a tree in the forest and stand it in a corner of the room —

especially when he found a big box of Christmas decorations tucked away in a cupboard under the stairs. Putting these up was fun, too. So was lighting the fire and laying the table for Christmas dinner.

After this King Wod drew a fancy Christmas card for the cottage owner. He stood it on the mantlepiece. Then, just in case, he made a fancy gift box as well. Inside he put a note saying:

"This space is reserved for a present from King Wod. It can be a book of answers to every question a teacher can ask, a picnic basket that glows in the dark for midnight feasts, a horse for riding on rainbows . . . anything you like. You choose."

And he put the gift box under the Christmas tree.

Last of all, for the best fun of all, he set out an extra place at the table. "Well," he sighed. "You never know . . ."

And he fell sound asleep in front of the fire.

It was daylight that woke him up. That and the sound of sleigh bells. The door swung open and in came just the sort of plump, comfy-looking old man you'd expect to live in a cottage like this. Mind you, with frost in his eyebrows, ice in his beard, and snowflakes melting on his red suit and empty sack, it took Wod at least two seconds to recognize him. "Santa Claus!" he gasped.

"Hello." said Santa Claus, "Who are you?"

"Er . . . King Wod, actually. I'm sorry about —"

"King Wod?"

Santa Claus stared at him in astonishment. "You mean that letter from the wizard was *real*? About how you were bringing me . . . bringing me . . ."

His voice trailed away as his eye fell on the decorations and the dinner table, the card on the mantlepiece, and the present under the tree.

"Oh, my goodness gracious!" he gasped. "How did you know?"

"Know?" said Wod. "Know what?"

"That I haven't had a proper Christmas *ever*."

"Haven't you?"

"Before it comes I'm always too busy. After it goes I'm always too tired. And now you've organized everything for me. Bless you, your Majesty! I'm so grateful. However did you think of such a lovely surprise present?"

"Surprise present?"

"My very own Christmas," said Santa Claus. "It's the first I've ever had."

"It's the first I've ever given," said King Wod, thoughtfully.

But already he knew it wouldn't be the last.

Wod never forgot the lesson his clever wizard had taught him. After all, if you're a king who's got everything, *receiving* a surprise present is bound to be difficult. But *giving* one is easy.

Later, after he'd made the wizard Prime Minister, King Wod said: "There is just one problem, though. What should I put in the box I left under the fir tree? Santa Claus couldn't decide which present he liked best."

"Simple," smiled the wizard.

And he whispered in King Wod's ear.

I'd love to tell you what he suggested. But that would spoil the surprise.

THE CHRISTMAS LION

Ann Jungman

As Christmas approached, the stores on Main Street began to pack their windows full of wonderful gifts. No store had a more beautiful window than the toy store.

In the middle of the toy store window was a magnificent green lion with bright red whiskers. His mane and his tail were thick and black. All around the lion were electronic toys, building blocks in bright colors, dolls, trains, games, things to make, and a huge selection of books. As Christmas came nearer, more and more of the things in the store were sold. But no one even asked about the magnificent green lion. He sat in the window and watched as the other toys were handled and chosen, packed in bright Christmas paper and taken away.

"No one wants to buy me," he said sadly to himself. "Still three more days to go though. Maybe someone will want me at the last minute."

But on Christmas Eve the lion still sat watching the window empty as parents rushed in to buy yet more last-minute presents. As it grew dark, he was almost the only toy left. The store was about to close. A tear ran down the lion's face.

"I'll have to spend Christmas all by myself," he thought.

The owner of the store looked at the lion. "That lion was a mistake," she said to her husband. "He was very expensive and I can't sell him."

"Mmmm, I can see why," replied her husband. "I mean, he's very splendid but he doesn't look very lovable."

"I'll reduce him in the sale," said the owner. "That may get rid of him."

The lion felt worse and worse.

At that moment an elegant woman dashed in. The lion looked at her very hard. "She must buy me," he said to himself in a determined whisper. "I won't let them put me in the sale. Just because I'm handsome doesn't mean I don't need someone to want me. What can I do to get her to like me? I know, I'll give her my nicest smile."

"I'm not too late, am I?" the woman gasped. "I need a present for my niece. She's five, I think."

"You could have this lion," said the shop owner quickly. "Any child would be thrilled with him."

The woman glanced at the lion. He smiled at her politely.

"I'll have him," she said. "I could swear he smiled at me just now." And she laughed.

So the lion was wrapped up and put on the back seat of a fast car. He lay there for the rest of the journey being bumped around and wondering what it would be like to be someone's toy at last.

Later that night, the lion was wrapped up in colored paper and put with the other presents under the Christmas tree. He fell asleep happily, feeling ordinary and wanted like any other toy.

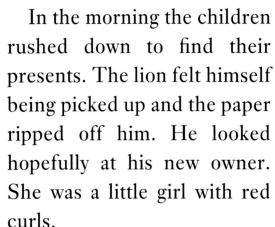

In the morning the children rushed down to find their presents. The lion felt himself being picked up and the paper ripped off him. He looked hopefully at his new owner. She was a little girl with red curls.

"I like the look of her," thought the lion cheerfully.

"Do you like your lion, Nicola?" asked the lady who had dashed into the shop.

"He's very nice, thank you Auntie Maggie," said Nicola, and she turned to open her other presents.

"Her name's Nicola," thought the lion. "I like that, it's a good name. I wonder what she'll call me?"

But Nicola didn't give the lion a name at all. She put him on a high shelf in her bedroom and took no more notice of him. The lion watched Nicola and her friends from his shelf. They seemed to enjoy playing with all the toys except him. He felt more lonely than ever.

"The shop owner must have been right," he said to himself. "I am very handsome, but I'm not very lovable. It's not much fun being handsome if nobody loves you."

The lion sat on the shelf gathering dust for months, and he became more and more unhappy. Then, one night, there was a great thunderstorm. The thunder crashed and the lightning flashed and the rain poured and poured. Slates fell off the roof of the house and, while Nicola slept, water began to leak into her room. The lion sitting on the top shelf was drenched through and through. The water completely changed the way the lion looked. No longer was he handsome and magnificent, he was now faded and crooked.

The next day, as Nicola's mother inspected the damage to the house, she came across the soaking wet lion. "Look," she said to Nicola. "Here's that funny old lion Auntie Maggie bought you for Christmas. He's had it. What a good thing you never liked him anyway. I'll throw him straight in the garbage can."

The lion had a moment of panic. "I'm going to be thrown away before I've ever had a friend to play with. Please don't let me be thrown away, Nicola. Please don't."

Tears fell down the lion's face. Nicola looked at him and then picked him up and gave him a big hug.

"No, Mom," said Nicola. "I want to keep him. He looks so sad all wet like that and his tail so droopy. Look, one ear's falling off and his eyes are all crooked. I like him like this. When he's dry I'm going to keep him at the end of my bed with teddy and the others."

"I see what you mean," said her mother. "Now that he doesn't look so new and expensive, he's really rather lovable."

From then on the lion was never lonely again. He lived at the end of the bed with the other toys, and whenever Nicola went out to sleep at a friend's house it was the lion she took for company. Her very special Christmas lion.

ALL I WANT FOR CHRISTMAS

Michael Morpurgo

On Christmas Eve in the afternoon, the snow began to fall. It was too good to believe. Alex ate his lunch as fast as he could.

"Can I get down, please?" he asked.

He found the tin tray under the sink.

"Remember to keep away from the stream Alex, that's all."

"Of course I will," said Alex.

His father was always warning him about that.

"And keep your hat and gloves on," said his mother, wrapping him up. "It's cold out there."

And it was too, but Alex hardly noticed it. With the tin tray under his arm he crunched through the snow to the top of Wood Hill. You could go faster if you lay flat on your stomach, and you could steer better that way too — that was what he thought anyway.

Alex lay down and gripped the tray. Then he let himself go. Before he knew it he was skimming over the snow, gathering speed all the time. He saw the mole hill too late.

The tray went one way and he went another. When at last he finished rolling and sliding, he stood up and looked for the tray. It was right at the bottom of the hill, by the stream, sticking

into the snow. He scrambled and slithered down the hill to pick it up. As he bent down, he saw something move out of the corner of his eye, blue and red, a flash of color against the white of the snow. It flew straight as an arrow and was gone. He crept closer and lay in the snow to watch.

Two kingfishers were perched on a branch over the stream. They took it in turns to fly off and dive at the ice. It was a moment or two before Alex understood what they were trying to do. He had seen them often enough in the summer diving for fish. Now with the stream iced over they were starving. They huddled together, one slightly bigger than the other, and looked at him.

Alex knew instantly what he had to do.

"Don't worry," he called out, "I'll make you a hole. It'll be all right."

He tried stones first, the biggest ones he could find. He lobbed them on to the ice, but they just bounced. So he  looked for heavier ones. They bounced too. From further up the stream he found a huge log. "This should do it," he said, but try as he might he couldn't lift it. The kingfishers watched

from their branch. He found a smaller log and tossed it as high as he could and it landed right where he wanted, bounced once and slid across the stream. There was not even a crack in the ice.

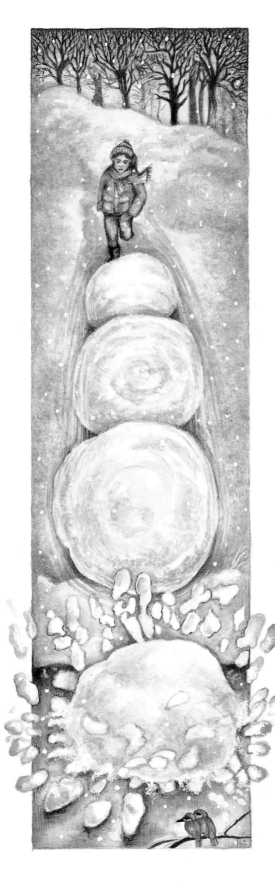

"Break! Why don't you break?" he shouted.

He picked up a handful of snow, squeezed it into a snowball and hurled it at the ice.

"Break! Why don't you break? Can't you see they're starving?"

He sat down on the bank and looked on hopelessly as the kingfishers dived again and again at the ice. He made another snowball, a bigger one this time, and threw it at the ice. It was no good. It was too small, but a bigger one! A giant one! That might do it!

He climbed right to the top of the hill and made it there, rolling it into a snowball as big as a tractor wheel, so big that by the time he had finished it he could only just move it. But that was all he needed to do. The hill did the rest.

The snowball thundered down the hill, bounced once up over the bank and crashed on to the ice. Alex ran down after it to see how big the hole was. But there was no

54

hole. The giant snowball, or all that was left of it, was spread all over the ice.

He heard his mother calling him in — it was almost dark by now.

"I'll think of something," he told the kingfishers.

But they looked away. They did not believe that any more than he did.

"Don't forget to put your stocking out for Santa Claus," said his father as he went upstairs to bed.

He would have forgotten, too. All he could think about was the starving kingfishers down by the frozen stream. He was hanging his stocking at the end of the bed when he had the idea. He always wrote a letter to Santa Claus, but this one would be different. He wrote in his best hand-writing:

Dear Santa Claus
Could you drive your sled down through the bottom of Wood Hill and break the ice for my kingfishers? They'll starve if you don't.
I've tried everything. I can't ask my Dad to help because then he will know that I've been near the stream and I'm not supposed to go there. So I'm asking you instead.
I won't have a happy Christmas if they starve and nor will they.
It's all I want for Christmas.
Love from Alex.

When he woke on Christmas Day, the letter was gone from the end of his bed and his stocking was stuffed full. He did not even stop to rummage inside. He put his coat on over his pajamas and ran outside. There were tracks and hoofprints on the path toward Wood Hill. He followed them all the way down the hill to the stream. Sure enough, the ice was broken and the kingfishers were darting back and forth. When they settled on their branch, Alex could see they had fish in their beaks. Up the hill on the other side of the stream the tracks disappeared. Alex looked up into the sky. "Thank you," he called out. "Thank you, Santa Claus."

"Well," said his father at breakfast, "did Santa Claus give you what you wanted?"

"'Course he did," said Alex. "He always does."

NO PETS – BY ORDER

Helen Cresswell

Jilly and Joe Potter knew very well what they wanted for Christmas. They also knew very well that they couldn't have it.

"A puppy, please," Jilly told Santa Claus when she visited him at the store.

"Or a kitten," added Joe. (He had gone in with Jilly because he was scared to go on his own. He was only four, and had never met Santa Claus before.)

"And what does your Mom say to that?" Santa Claus's eyes were bright under his snow-white brows.

"She says we can't," Jilly told him. "Pets not allowed, she says."

"You'd better tell me what else you'd like, then," said Santa Claus.

So Jilly and Joe told him about the train set and the fire engine. He listened and nodded, then gave Jilly a jigsaw and Joe a coloring book and crayons, and said goodbye.

The reason why Jilly and Joe could not have their puppy or kitten was that they lived in an apartment house. No pets allowed — that was one of the rules.

"We're lucky to be on the first floor," Mom told them. "At least you have somewhere to play." There was a patch of grass and a lilac tree and a laurel bush.

"Well, did you tell Santa what toys you'd like?" Mom asked.

"We told him about the puppy and the kitten," Joe said.

"Because Santa's magic," Jilly explained. "He doesn't have to go by rules."

"I'm afraid he does, Jilly," Mom told her. "No pets. Even Santa can't do anything about *that* rule."

"Is it against the rules to drive sleds and reindeer in the sky?" asked Jilly.

Mom laughed. "I expect so."

"There you are then!" said Jilly.

On Christmas Eve Joe and Jilly hung up their stockings. Mom came in to say goodnight.

"Now straight to sleep!" she told them. "Or Santa won't come!" She switched on the night light in the shape of a toadstool and went out. Jilly heard her go into the living room. Then she heard a carol — *While Shepherds Watched*. She climbed out of bed.

"What are you doing?" whispered Joe.

"Getting this." She pulled open a drawer and took something out.

"What is it?"

"A rubber bone! For our puppy!" Jilly had bought it weeks ago from the pet shop down the road.

"Silly Jilly!" said Joe. "No puppy. Against the rules. 'Night, silly Jilly!" And he closed his eyes.

Jilly placed the rubber bone by her stocking, and got back into bed.

"Jilly! Jilly!" Joe was tugging her sleeve.

"Wake up — it's Christmas!"

She sat up and her eyes went straight to her stocking. It was bulging with all kinds of exciting things, but Jilly hardly saw them.

"The puppy!" she wailed. "No puppy!"

"'Course not!" said Joe. He ran to his own stocking and started pulling things out. After a moment, Jilly did the same.

One by one they pulled out their toys with shrieks of delight. There were games, tricks, trumpets, candy. It was only when they had emptied the stockings that they saw the two big boxes — one each. A train set for Jilly and a fire engine for Joe.

"Hurray!" yelled Joe. "Hurray for Santa!"

Then Mom came in and had to be shown everything. It was she who spotted the crumpled paper right in the toe of Jilly's stocking.

"Look — what's that?"

Jilly pulled out the paper. There was a message printed on it in big letters. She spelled it out slowly.

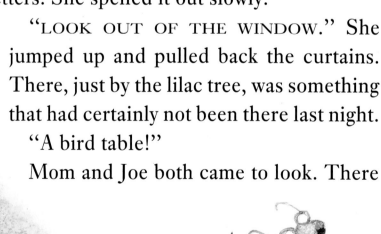

"LOOK OUT OF THE WINDOW." She jumped up and pulled back the curtains. There, just by the lilac tree, was something that had certainly not been there last night.

"A bird table!"

Mom and Joe both came to look. There

was a bag of nuts hanging from the table, and on it were crusts and crumbs. As they watched, a robin flew down.

"A Christmas robin!" Jilly was enchanted. They watched him tilt his head from side to side, pecking.

"You know what I think?" Mom said. "I think that Santa Claus has sent you that robin as a pet. *That's* not against the rules!"

"I'm going to make him really tame!" said Jilly. "I'm going to get him so tame that he'll come and eat out of my hand!"

She did, too. Other birds came to the table, of course — blue tits, sparrows, starlings, and thrushes, but the robin was always Jilly's favorite.

"Nobody else I know had a real live robin from Santa for Christmas," she said. And as for the rubber bone — she gave it to Joe, to play with in his bath!

THE SILVER CUP

Joan Aiken

Joe's daily run for the newspaper took seven minutes. Two minutes up the sandy lane, one more to the paper shop and back, three talking to Mr. Stubbs, one running home downhill.

Mr. Stubbs, an old sailor, swept the village street with a broom and long-handled pan. "I like to be out every day talking to people," he said.

One morning Joe asked him about a pile of stones and sand in a plastic sack which had lain outside the post office for weeks.

"Post office folk left it," said Mr. Stubbs. "I shan't touch it. Let 'em take it. Maybe if I shifted it, they'd turn me into a toad."

Another time, Joe asked about the two white-painted posts outside the Green Dragon inn, which had been knocked flat in the night.

"Maybe the Green Dragon did it," said Mr. Stubbs.

A month before Christmas, Joe noticed a silvery metal cup wedged into the sandy bank at the corner where the lane met the village street.

"What do you think that is?" said Joe.

Mr. Stubbs puffed out his white moustache thoughtfully.

Today was very cold. Frost silvered the grass like sugar on strawberries. Mr. Stubbs had on his blue knitted cap. His nose was red as a strawberry.

"Tell you what," he said at last. "I think Santa Claus put that there for someone to make him a Christmas pudden."

"He did?" Joe was surprised. "Why?"

"He got no time to make his own, does he? Always driving around with those reindeer."

"But," said Joe, "Christmas only comes once a year."

"Ah? *Here* that's so. But what about in space?" said Mr. Stubbs. "What about out there? It's always Christmas somewhere, out there. Old Sandy Claws is at it the whole year long, dashing from one star to another. And the planets. And the sun. All those moons. *He* don't get no three weeks' vacation."

"You think we ought to make him a Christmas pudding?" said Joe.

"I do," said Mr. Stubbs.

"I'll ask Mom," said Joe.

Next day he told Mr. Stubbs, "Mom says we can make a Christmas pudding if I can wash that cup really clean." He lifted the sandy metal cup out of the tuft of grass where it had lodged. "Mind you, Dad says it's only a hubcap."

"Ah," said Mr. Stubbs. "Off the sleigh, likely."

"Do sleighs have hubcaps?"

"Those that run on ball bearings do." Mr. Stubbs sniffed the frosty air. "Going to be a white Christmas. The birds think so, and they know."

"Why?"

"Cousins of Sandy Claws, they be. All that Claws family know about the weather. They know where it comes from. You can see 'em fly off the other way." He pointed. "See, the sky's all black in the north. And the birds is going south."

Joe took the silver cup home and rubbed and scrubbed and scraped it until his Mom said it was clean enough to put Christmas pudding mix in.

She had been beating up eggs and milk and flour and butter and raisins and currants and candied peel and nutmeg and cinnamon and allspice and brandy; and, as well, she had dropped in a thin, worn, old, silver penny piece, more than a hundred years old, which had belonged to Joe's great-granny. "For luck," she said. "Whoever finds it in his helping gets a wish."

"Even if Santa Claus finds it?"

"Of course."

When they had all stirred the gooey pudding mix it was spooned into three big bowls and also the metal cup that Joe had brought home. Wax paper was laid on top, and cloths tied over, and the puddings were boiled for hours.

"When will they be done?" Joe kept saying, and Mom kept saying, "Not yet. Christmas pudding has to be cooked for a really long time."

The smell in the house while the puddings were cooking was so dark and rich and strong that you could have eaten the air with a spoon.

Outside, the birds had become quiet. It was growing colder and colder. Every morning Joe scattered crumbs. Birds would come with a swish and flutter. Every crumb would be gone before Joe was back in the kitchen.

Smoke went straight up from the chimney, like a line ruled to the middle of the sky. The ground was hard as brick.

"Soon it'll snow," said Mr. Stubbs.

But it didn't; not yet.

The puddings were put away at the back of the pantry, with the little one in its silver cup.

At last came Christmas Eve. Joe and his Dad walked to the woods and cut branches of holly and pine. They were stiff and rustly and smelt of magic. There was a sprig of mistletoe, with waxy white berries like pearls. And the Christmas tree was in a tub, ready to be hung with lights and shining balls. But that would not happen till Joe was in bed.

He hung up his stocking.

"Now can I leave Santa's pudding for him?" he asked.

"Wrap up warm and run fast, then," said Mom, "for it's colder than I've ever known."

Dad went with Joe. It was dark. They could feel the frost crunch under their boots. The air was full of bell-music; tingle-tangle, dingle-dangle, ding-dong, dong, dong.

"You'd think the air would break in splinters," said Joe, sniffing its iciness.

The silver cupful of Christmas pudding was hidden carefully in the middle of a tuft of frosty grass.

"Will he be able to find it?" said Joe.

"Certain to," said Dad. "Let's run all the way home."

Next morning there was still no snow.

After undoing his stocking, and after breakfast but before the presents on the tree were opened, Joe raced up the lane. There would be no newspaper, of course, on Christmas Day, but he wanted to see if Santa Claus had taken the pudding.

As Joe reached the village street, a few snowflakes began to fall. The sun, very low and red, had been trying to shine, but now it snuggled into a cloud, as if it had decided to go back to bed.

There was Mr. Stubbs, with his broom.

"On Christmas Day?" said Joe, very surprised, but Mr. Stubbs said, "People stay out late, Christmas Eve, and leave all kinds of rubbish. That's not nice for Christmas Day."

And he dropped two cans and a chip bag into his pan.

Joe ran to the tussock where he and Dad had put the pudding, and found the cup was gone. There was a round dent where it had been.

He felt pleased, but also a little worried.

"It's gone," he said, "but how do we *know* that Santa took it? Perhaps those people who dropped the cans might have found it."

"Humph," said Mr. Stubbs, tugging his moustache, staring at the sky. "That's true. How *do* we know? That's a hard one."

But then he said, "Hey — boy! Look at the sky!"

Joe looked at the sky. The sun was still nestled behind a round, dark cloud. And out of the cloud, and other scattered clouds, flakes of snow, black and busy as bees, were pouring down.

And around the cloud, all the way around, like a flaming, many-colored collar, there ran a rainbow. A complete circle of rainbow, bright and glowing.

"Well, blow me!" said Mr. Stubbs. "A whole, round rainbow. I never in all my life at sea saw *that!*"

The snow pelted down, whitening the ground, and the rainbow hung, flashing, and the man and the boy stood staring at it. Gradually it faded, as the snow fell thicker and thicker.

"Well," said Mr. Stubbs, "reckon that was from old Sandy Claws to say thank you for his pudden. Now I'm off home, for I can't sweep up all this snow. And you'd best get back to your presents."

So Joe raced home down the lane, holding the rainbow inside his mind, like a silver cup.

The Christmas Mouse

Sarah Hayes

Fenny was a little brown mouse with soft velvety fur and eyes like black beads. She lived in a hole in the baseboard.

Every night, as soon as the house was quiet, Fenny would creep out of her hole and run across the carpet to an old brown armchair. A small boy called Tom often sat there, and sometimes Fenny found cooky crumbs he had dropped, or even flakes of chocolate. But sometimes there were no crumbs, and Fenny would have to go home hungry.

One night Fenny crept out of her hole to find everything changed. Leaves hung from the walls, and the ceiling was covered with colored paper. The old brown armchair was gone, and in its place stood a prickly green tree sparkling with lights. Under the tree lay a great mound of packages. She tweaked a piece of ribbon and jumped back in fright as the bow untied itself and the wrapping paper sprang open.

Fenny's whiskers twitched: she could smell something nice on the prickly tree. She clambered on to a low branch, and scurried past a blue bird and a wooden angel playing a drum. She sniffed. Then she stood on tiptoe and nibbled a gingerbread heart which hung from the branch above her. It tasted good. She ate some more. All of sudden she lost her balance. The branch rocked and several things fell onto the ground. Fenny had to jump down very quickly.

Near the prickly tree was a low table with a group of strange objects on it. Fenny was a curious mouse, so she climbed up to have a look. She touched one of the objects: it was hard and cold. Then she noticed something that looked like a little bed right in the middle of the group. It was not hard and cold like the other things. It was made of wood and filled with soft hay, and it was just the right size for a mouse. Fenny yawned. The little mouse bed looked very

inviting. She yawned again. Then she climbed into the hay. There was someone else in the little bed, but Fenny didn't mind. She curled up in a ball and went fast asleep.

Early in the morning, before the grown-ups were awake, a small boy came into the living room. It was Tom, and he was in his pajamas. Tom stood and gazed at the packages under the tree. He saw that the wrapping paper had come undone on one of the presents, and he saw that the end of the gingerbread heart had been nibbled off. Several ornaments had fallen off the tree.

Then Tom caught his breath. He thought he saw something moving on the low table. He knelt down to look and gasped. Someone was curled up fast asleep beside baby Jesus in the manger — someone with twitching whiskers and brown velvety fur.

"A Christmas mouse," whispered Tom, and Fenny woke up. For a moment the tiny black bead eyes stared into Tom's large brown ones. Then Fenny scrambled out of the manger and jumped off the table. She raced around the room, under the prickly tree, over the mound of presents, across the carpet and back to her hole in the baseboard.

Fenny never slept in the little mouse bed again, and in a few days it was taken away, along with the prickly tree and the colored paper on the ceiling. The old brown armchair returned to its place, and all was just as it had been before. Except for one thing. Every night, when Fenny came out of her hole, a little pile of crumbs was waiting for her on the low table. Sometimes there were breadcrumbs, sometimes bits of cheese or nuts. And once in a while there were tiny mouse-sized pieces of chocolate. But Tom never forgot to feed the mouse who had slept in the manger on Christmas night. And Fenny never went home hungry ever again.

A TROUBLESOME YEAR FOR SANTA CLAUS

Sally Grindley

One year nothing went right for Santa Claus. To begin with, the mice had been nibbling at his sacks, so they were all full of holes and the toys fell through. Then he found that the elves had been growing geraniums in his Christmas-best boots. The elf children had used up all his notepads for coloring, so he hadn't any paper to write thank you notes to people who left him mince pies. And when he jumped into his sleigh, he slid on an egg that one of his hens had laid there.

He finally set off an hour late and with the grumbles of his reindeer ringing in his ears. They all had colds and were feeling very sorry for themselves. Santa Claus had to make them fly faster than usual to make up for lost time. He didn't dare think about what would happen if he hadn't visited every child throughout the world before morning.

They sped through the air, bells ringing loudly, and reached the first houses in double-quick time. Santa Claus slid down the chimneys like a fireman down his pole, and filled every stocking lying alongside every sleeping child. Then off they went again, to the next village, the next town, the next city, on and on until . . .

Rudolph's nose went out. Suddenly it was very, very dark. They were in the middle of nowhere and there were no lights from the ground to guide them. The reindeer came to a halt.

"What's the matter, Rudolph?" said Santa Claus.

"It's dis cold in me dose," said Rudolph. "It's made me dose stop shining."

"Bother my boots," said Santa Claus. "Bother my belt and braces." He fiddled around at the front of the sleigh and found a small flashlight. When he switched it on, a thin line of light streamed out in front of him.

"Bother my beard," said Santa Claus. "This is all

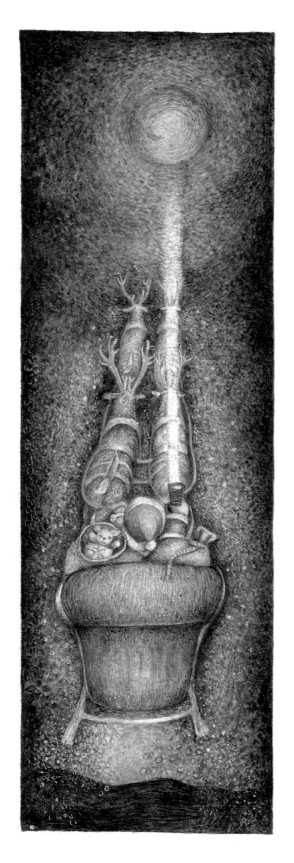

the light we've got, and it won't last long. There's only one thing for it, we'll have to wake up the Man in the Moon."

As soon as he said it a loud groan came from all the reindeer. It was bad enough flying around the world with a bad cold, let alone paying a visit to the Man in the Moon on the way. Beside, he always looked so grumpy.

"Come on now," said Santa Claus. "We must get going. We're late enough already."

He steered the sleigh away from the earth and up, up, up they flew, the thin light from the flashlight guiding them toward the very faint circle in the distance. It didn't take long. It was much quicker to go to the moon than to travel all the way around the earth. When they reached the landing platform, Santa Claus tumbled out and ran to the Man in the Moon's front door. He knocked loudly.

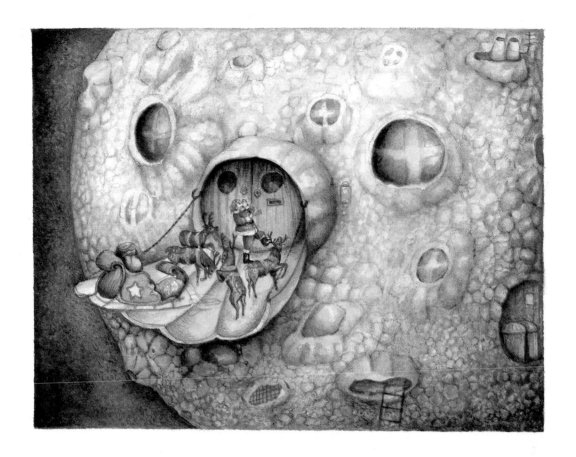

There was no reply. He knocked again. Still no reply. A loud rumbly snore echoed around the house.

"Bother my bootlaces," said Santa Claus. "We'll never wake him up."

The reindeer stood miserably sniffing and shuffling their feet.

"Come on now, reindeer," said Santa Claus. "I want you all to stamp your hooves, whinny as loudly as you can, and dance around to make your bells ring."

"But what about our sore throats?" protested Rudolph.

"Never mind your sore throats," said Santa Claus. "This is an emergency!"

The reindeer did as they were told. The noise was

tremendous. Santa Claus joined in by going HO HO HO! as loudly as he could and blowing the horn on the sleigh.

Suddenly, a light went on somewhere in the house, and a grumpy voice bellowed through the letterbox. "What's going on? Who the dickens is making all that racket? Who dares to wake me up on one of my few days off? Speak up!"

"I'm terribly sorry," said Santa Claus, "but we need your help. I'm Santa Claus and I'm on my way around the world delivering presents. But Rudolph's shiny nose has gone out and we can't see where we're going."

The door of the house opened and a huge, bad-tempered

man appeared. "I suppose you want me to work, do you?" said the Man in the Moon. "You come here and wake me up with all your racket, and now you want me to work. Why should I?"

Santa Claus took a deep breath and the reindeer tossed their heads uneasily. "A lot of children will be very unhappy if they wake up to empty stockings tomorrow morning," said Santa Claus.

"Nobody ever gave me a present," grumbled the Man in the Moon. "Never. Not even a Christmas card. I hate Christmas. That's why I always sleep on Christmas Eve instead of working."

Santa Claus listened sympathetically, and then he had an idea. "I tell you what," he said. "I'll bring you presents. I'll come here with my reindeer every year after we've been around the world, and we'll eat mince pies and talk and you can open presents in front of the fire. But in return you must promise always to work on Christmas Eve so that I'll always be able to find my way."

Try as he might to keep on his grumpy face, a twinkle appeared in the Man in the Moon's eye.

"Do you mean it?" he said.

"Go to work now," said Santa Claus, "and I'll join you for breakfast in the morning and give you your presents."

The Man in the Moon disappeared indoors without another word. Suddenly, the whole place was bathed in bright light. The reindeer screwed up their eyes, half blinded. Santa Claus jumped back into his sleigh.

"Come on," he said. "Full speed ahead. No time to lose."

And off they went, down, down, down, until they could see the tops of trees and buildings again. When Santa Claus looked back, there was the Moon shining brightly, and there was the face of the Man in the Moon smiling broadly.

Santa Claus just managed to finish delivering presents on time that year. Then he went back to the moon and shared mince pies and brandy with the Man in the Moon and left him his presents. He finally arrived back at the North Pole at lunchtime on Christmas Day. He sent his reindeer off to a health farm for a week, and settled down for a nice long sleep.

The Man in the Moon always works on Christmas Eve now and, as you will see, he has a smile on his face all year long.